Dedicated to my family and my fur babies.

Library of Congress Cataloging-in-Publication Data available

ISBN 978-1-338-56542-3

10 9 8 7 6 5 4 3 2 1   20 21 22 23 24

Printed in China   38
First edition, August 2020

Book design by Steve Ponzo

ISABELLA KUNG

NO FUZZBALL!

Orchard Books
An Imprint of Scholastic Inc. • New York

Hello, I am
NoFuzzball.

Perhaps you have never heard a name like this before,
but that is because you have not met
a **queen** like me.

My subjects *worship* me.
Hear how they scream my name
everywhere I go . . .

We live in my **queendom** in total harmony.

See how my subjects do all my bidding.

They **entertain** me,

feed me,
groom me,
massage me,

and shower me with **presents**!

Oh look.
A new gift!

What a perfect **queen**-sized bed!

Ugh, sometimes
they can be a
little too clingy.

They messed up
my **royal** coat.

A queen cannot tolerate such disrespect!
I demand a formal apology . . .

Wait, they left?

How dare they
forget their place?!

What has gotten into them?

Ahh . . . yes, of course! My subjects must be so ashamed of their behavior, they went to find the perfect royal offerings for me.

Glad they took that disgusting slobbering mess, too.
Finally, some peace and quiet! Time for . . .

...some uninterrupted **beauty sleep.**

That nap was divine!

Now, where is that personal masseuse of mine? She knows I must have my daily massages!

yawn

Hello!
I am awake now!

They are still gone?

Where did they go??

They have never been
away this long . . .

They are not that smart . . .

What if they are lost?
Or hurt?

Maybe someone captured them?!

What if . . .

. . . they just don't want to live
in my **queendom** anymore?

I know! I will be a charitable ruler.
I will make them the finest beds!

Share my fanciest toys!

Spoil them with the greatest gifts!
Nothing is too good for my subjects!

They are **family!**

I'll need to redecorate
the palace, too.

I must redesign
the racetrack,

carve out the
best napping areas,

and freshen things up
with my signature style!

They are going to love
my **royal renovations!**

RUFF
RUFF

What is that noise?
My subjects have returned home?

Wait, what did they call me?!

Has it been so long?
They have forgotten their
queen's name is . . .

Aw . . .
they LOVE me.

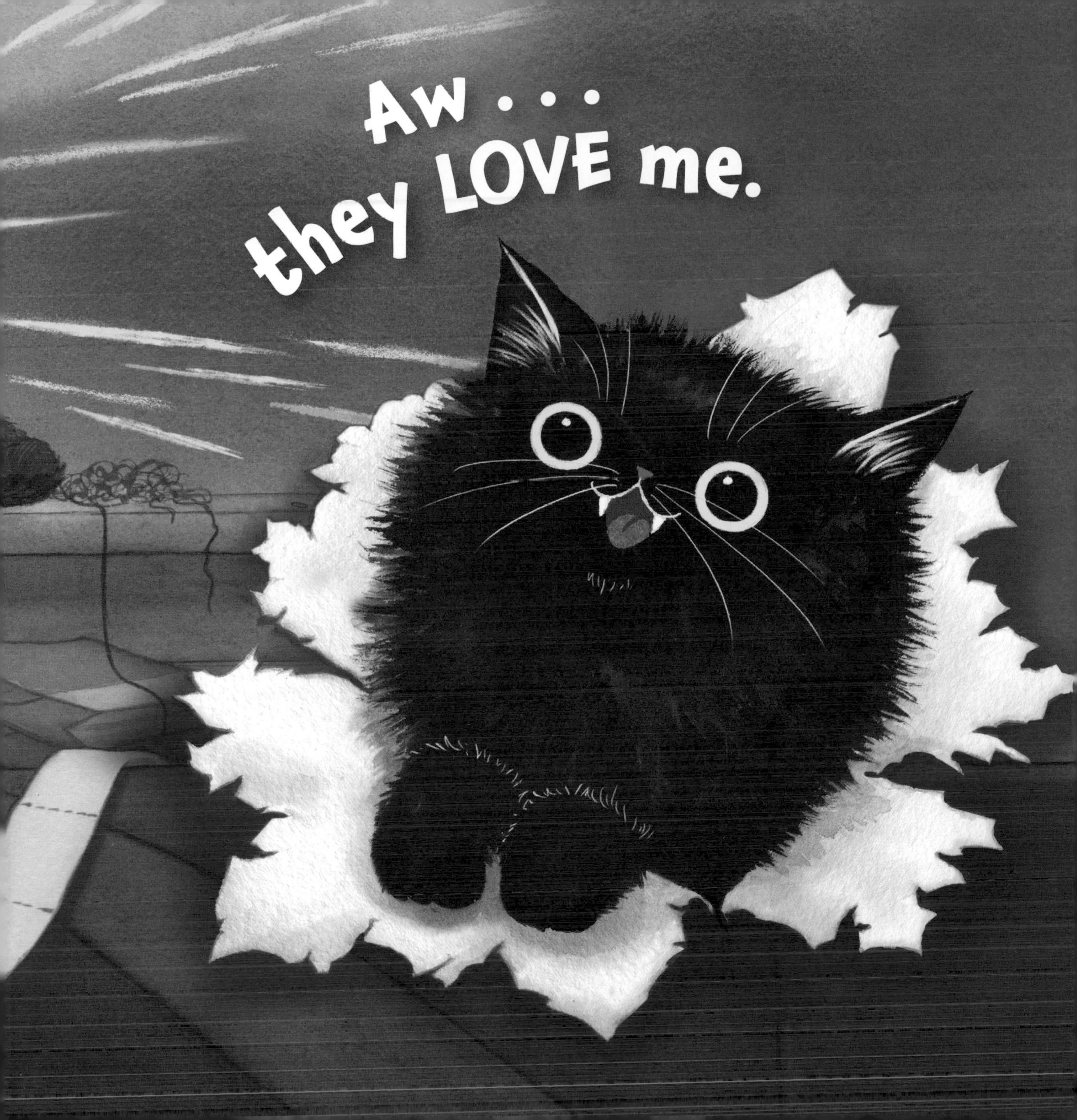